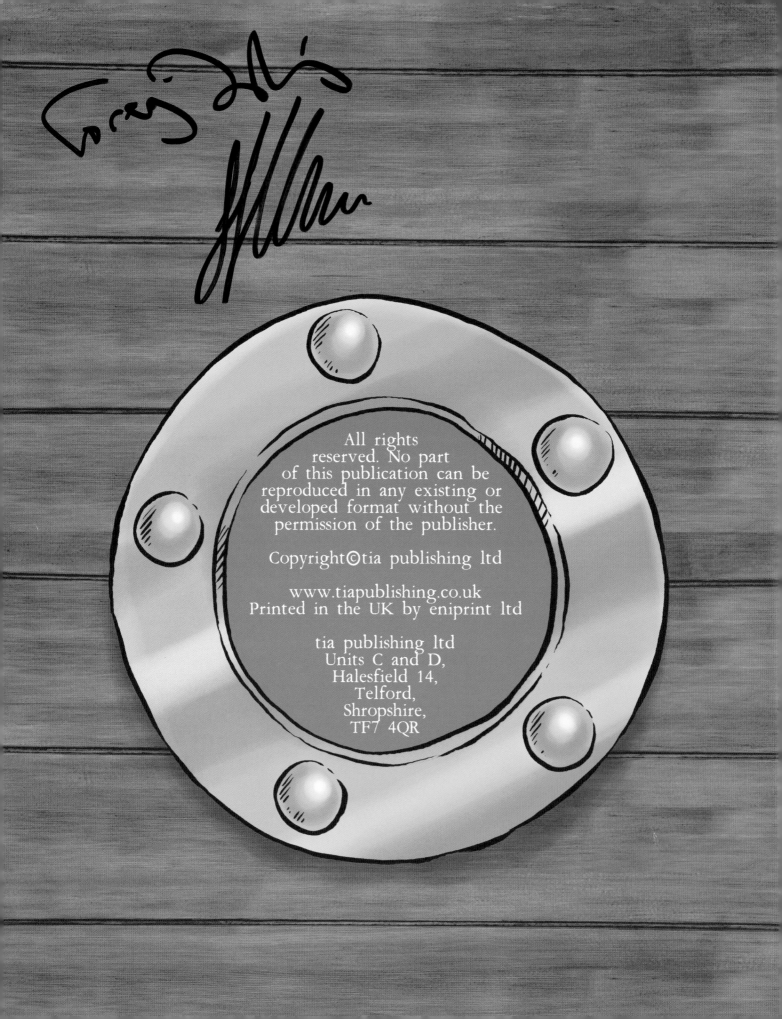

www.tiapublishing.co.uk
Printed in the UK by eniprint ltd

tia publishing ltd
Units C and D,
Halesfield 14,
Telford,
Shropshire,
TF7 4QR

The Positively Pleasant Pirates

written by Greg Dobbins

illustrated by Simon Norse

A jolly Pirate and his swashbuckling crew,
set sail for adventure on the **ocean blue**.

Now most other pirates are nasty and mean,
the most selfish men that you've ever seen.
But this jolly Pirate was ever so caring;
unlike other pirates he was happy with **sharing**.

The waves they rolled, and the winds they blew.

On sailed the Pirate and his swashbuckling crew.

"Oh Crew!"
called the Pirate,
his spirits
rising.

"I
see a ship,
there on the
horizon"

They sailed alongside and cheered as they boarded.

Then looked to see what treasure was hoarded.

Ahoy and Avast! Treasure at last!

The waves they rolled,
and the winds they blew.

On sailed the Pirate
and his swashbuckling crew.

"Oh Crew!"
called the Pirate, getting excited.
"I see a ship, the second I've sighted."

They sailed alongside and cheered as they boarded, then looked to see what treasure was

hoarded.

Ahoy and Avast! Treasure at last!

"I say," said the Pirate, looking around. "Would you please share any treasure you've found?"

"Such polite Pirates,
it would be a pleasure,
to give you just
a bit of our treasure.

Look in the hold,
there's a big crate of vests,
leave us a dozen,
and you take the rest."

The waves they rolled,
and the winds they blew.
On sailed the Pirate
and his swashbuckling crew.

"Oh Crew!"

called the Pirate,
jumping with glee.
"I spy a ship,
I think that makes three."

They sailed alongside
and cheered as they boarded,
then looked to see
what treasure was hoarded.

Ahoy and Avast!
Treasure at last!

The waves they rolled,
and the winds they blew.
On sailed the Pirate
and his swashbuckling crew.

"Oh Crew!" called the Pirate,

"D'you know what I'm thinking?
That ship over there
looks like it's sinking!"

"Help!" cried the crew
of the other boat.
"Our cargo's too heavy,
we can't stay afloat!"

They pulled and pulled, but to no avail. "Let's use the vests as an extra sail!"

Then the sails billowed
and the wind blew,
and into the safety
of harbour they
flew.

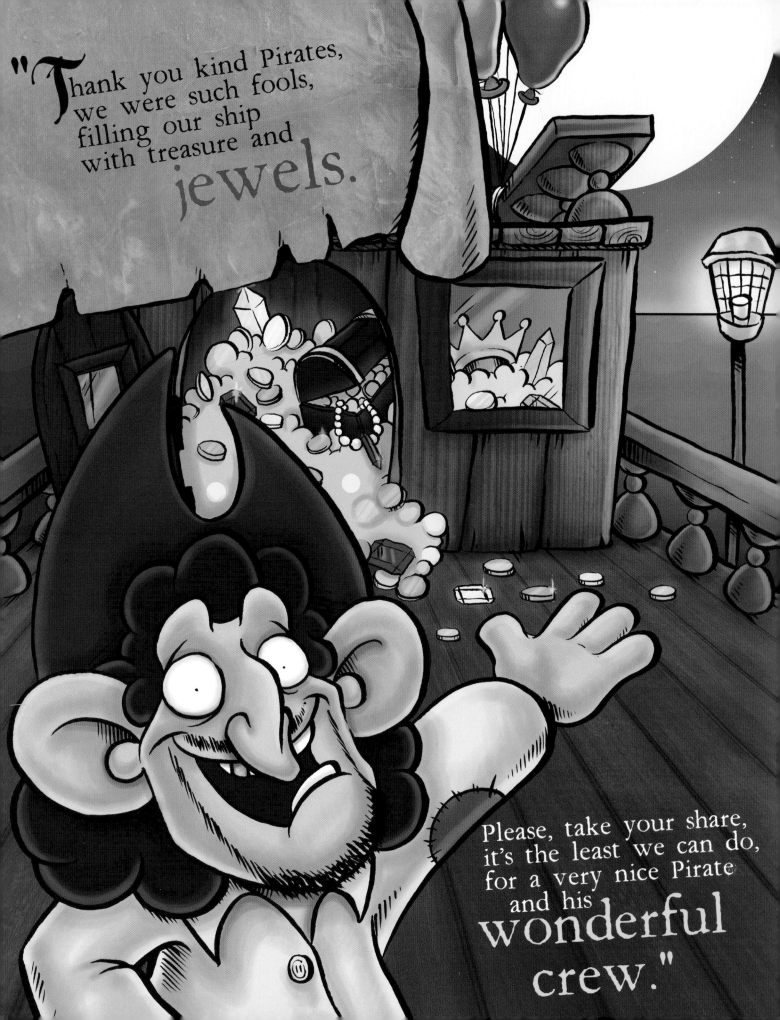

What can you remember?

What did the polite pirates get from the first pirate they met?

What did the polite pirates use to make an extra sail?

How did the crew feel about the treasure from the first 3 boats?

What colour was the octopus on the 3rd pirate ship?

What is different about the positively pleasant pirates?

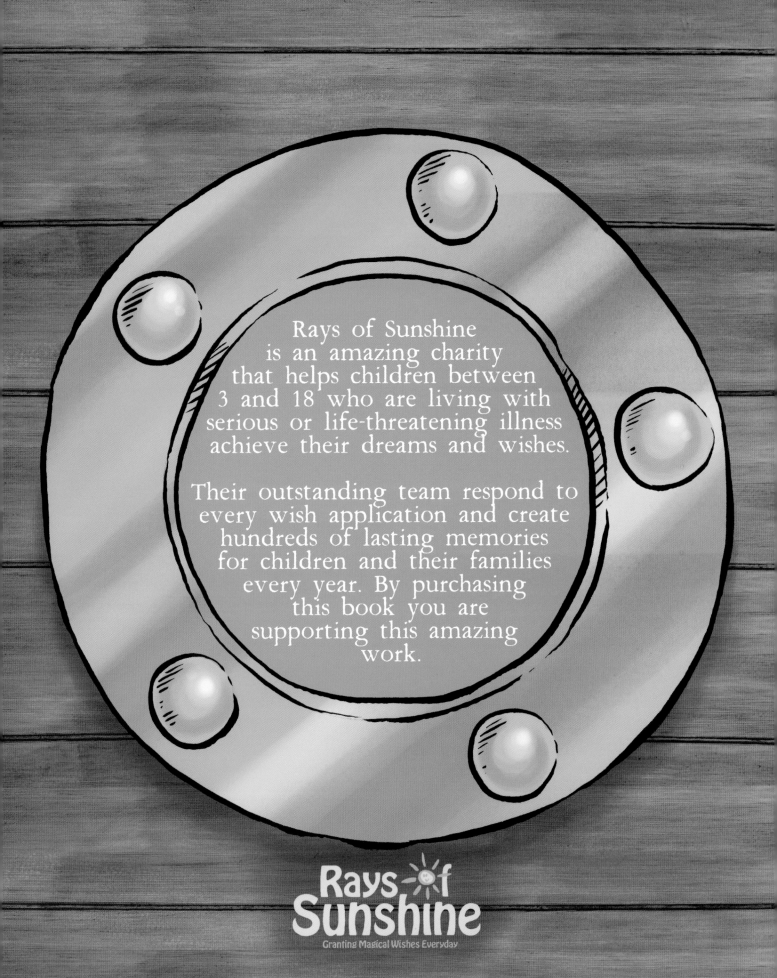

Rays of Sunshine
is an amazing charity
that helps children between
3 and 18 who are living with
serious or life-threatening illness
achieve their dreams and wishes.

Their outstanding team respond to
every wish application and create
hundreds of lasting memories
for children and their families
every year. By purchasing
this book you are
supporting this amazing
work.

Rays of Sunshine
Granting Magical Wishes Everyday